STORY AND ART BY

Sankichi Hinodeya

CONTENTS

#8:HERO
MODE
PART 1

HURRAY!
I MADE IT ON TIME TODAY!!
GOGGLES
MORNING, RIDER!!
GRAB
ARE YOU PRACTIC-ING TODAY TOO, RIDER?
Aw! You're too quick!
...

WHAT, EXACTLY, DID YOU MAKE IT ON TIME FOR?
RIDER
HA HA!
SHWING
I ACTUALLY MANAGED TO GET HERE ON TIME FOR THE TEAM MEETING!!
SO YOU'RE USUALLY LATE FOR IT, HUH.
OH? THE OTHERS AREN'T HERE.
AH!
BAAM
WE DON'T HAVE PRACTICE TODAY...!!
I forgot...
YOU DUMMY!!
Oh well.
I'LL JUST HAVE LUNCH THEN.
YOU WANT SOME?
NO.
KL
INK

GLEEEAM
SHOOT
HOOK!!
FWUMP
MY RICE BALL!!
WHOA!!
!
UH?
HUH?

FWEEE
AAAAAAAH!
EEE
AAAAAAAH!
PLIP
OH?
!

OCTO
PUS
OCTOPUS?

KR
CHK
KRCHK?
SPLUB SPLUB SPLUB SPLUB SPLUB
AAAAAH!
THEY'RE ATTACKING US!
THEY'RE OCTO-TROOPERS!
WHAT ARE THEY?!
!
SPLUB
SPLUB
SPLUB SPLUB SPLUB

BAAAM
LITTLE HELP?!
RIDER!
WHAT ARE YOU DOING UP THERE?!
FINE.
SPLUB
SPLUB
YEEHAAH!!
OOH!!

Pheeew
THANKS!
I ALWAYS KNEW YOU TWO COULD DO IT.
Phew.
YOU WERE IMPRESSIVE TOO, DYNAMO!
ALWAYS KNEW?
WHO ARE YOU, OLD MAN?

BUM
BAAA
I'M CAP'N CUTTLEFISH, LEADER OF THE LEGENDARY SQUIDBEAK SPLATOON!
AND I NEED YOUR HELP!

WHAT A FINE-LOOKING BEARD!
COOL, ISN'T IT?
STAY ON TOPIC!
THIS IS OCTO VALLEY, LOCATED UNDERNEATH INKOPOLIS.
IT'S THE HOME OF THE OCTARIANS. THE OCTOPUS ARMY!

THEY HAVE STOLEN THE ZAPFISH, EVEN THE GREAT ZAPFISH, FROM THE SURFACE...
...AND THEY'RE GOING TO USE THEM TO POWER AN INVASION.
IT'S AN EMERGENCY!!
PLEASE!
I NEED YOU TO GET THE GREAT ZAPFISH BACK!!
I'll throw in these crabby cakes too.
I DON'T HAVE ANY PRACTICE TODAY, SO WHY NOT?!
These crabby cakes are good.
HEY...!
BUT THIS OL' MAN HERE'S IN TROUBLE.
...FINE.
OOH!
THEN...

STARTING TODAY, YOU ARE AGENT 3 OF THE NEW SQUIDBEAK SPLATOON...
...AND AGENT 3.5!!
POINT FIVE?
TA-DAAAAH
COOL!
THEN THERE'S AN AGENT 1 AND AN AGENT 2 AS WELL?
YEP. YOUR UNIFORMS ARE THEIR HAND-ME-DOWNS.
HAND-ME-DOWNS...!
I've set the ink color to Agent 3
SHFF
WOOSH
WHA-?!

DRAT!
THEY'RE COMIN' OUT OF THE KETTLES AGAIN!!
SPLUB!
STOP THEM!!
AT THIS RATE, THEY'LL START INVADING THE SURFACE!
OKAY!
HUMPH.
LET'S DO IT!!
SPLUB SPLUB SPLUB

SPLASH!
THAT'S IT!
SPLUB SPLUB SPLUB SPLUB
SPLUB
WELL DONE...
...YOU TWO!!
SPLUB SPLUB
TEE HEE!
TEE HEE!
I got loose!
!
GET DOWN FROM THERE!!
Gah!
I'M STUCK ON ITS SUCKER!

THESE INKLINGS ARE STUPIDER THAN I THOUGHT.
Tee hee
Tee hee
STUPID.
HUH?!
HUMANOID FORMS!!
THEY'RE OCTOLINGS!!
HEY, OCTOLINGS!!
!
COOL GOGGLES!
WHY WOULD YOU SAY THAT!?
HUH.
FLATTERY WILL GET YOU NOWHERE, SQUID!
BLUSH
YOU'RE BLUSH-ING.
BLUSH
SH...
SHUT UP!!

SPLUB
SPLUB SPLUB
DEFEAT THE SQUIDS!!
THEY'RE ATTACK-ING!!
IT'S TWO AGAINST ONE!!
YOU CAN'T DODGE ALL OF OUR ATTACKS!!
SPLUB SPLUB
GOGGLES!!
I GOT THIS!!

SQUID LIGHT-NING JET!!
!
AAH!!
SPLUB SPLUB SPLUB
!

SPLISH
AAAH!
ACK...!
HOW DARE YOU!
SPLASH
OH.
SHE ESCAPED.
NAAH AAH!
HUH?
C'MON IN!
YOU'RE MISSING OUT IF YOU DON'T. IT'S UH—A LOT OF *FUN* IN HERE!
IT'S A TRAP.

SOUNDS GREAT!
Wait for me!
DOO-OOON'T!
HMPH!
BOOP BOOP
WHOOOOAA!!

BLADOOM!
HEH.
IT'S HUUUGE!!
!
WHAT IS IT ?!
GOGGLES, LOOK!

HA HA HA!
ZZLL
SH
IT IS!!
IT'S THE ZAPFISH!!
THIS IS THE *MIGHTY OCTOSTOMP.*
GLARE
WOA
I WILL CRUSH YOU!!
AAAAAH!!
OOSH

VRA-
DOOM
THAT WAS CLOSE.
ZZZZP
QUICK, WHILE IT'S DOWN!
SHOOT THE TENTACLE!
THAT THING?!
SLO
FINE!
I'LL DO IT!!
OSH

SPLOOSH
URRGH ...!
NICE WORK, RIDER!!
TCH.
THAT WAS EASY.
RIDER, LOOK OUT!!
WHA-?
AAAAAH!
KRA
!
DOOM
YOU MONSTER !!

BLAAM
I'LL AVENGE YOU, RIDER!!
I'M DOWN HERE!!
PHEEW
I THOUGHT YOU'D BECOME FLAT RIDER!
SPLAT
WHAT ARE YOU BABBLING ABOUT?! Flat Rider?!
IT'S NOT OVER YET, BOYS!!
YOU'VE STILL GOT ANOTHER ROUND AGAINST IT!!
RRMB
WHAT?
HUH?

KRA-
AAAAH!!
DOOM
IT'S STILL GOING!
HA HA HA.
YOU CAN'T DEFEAT IT THAT EASILY.
THERE'S NO SPACE LEFT!!
I can't paint it!
TCH!
PL
IP
I'LL TAKE CARE OF IT IN JUST...
WHAT?
FWOOM
AAAARGH!!
AAAH!
RIDER!!
FWOOM
GL
I HAVE A PLAN!
OMP
?!

LET GO OF RIDER!!
TICKLE TICKLE
THAT'LL NEVER WORK!
TICKLE
RATTLE RATTLE
IT'S WORK-ING!!
BUT ITS TENTACLE STILL HAS ME!!
KLAK
THEN I'LL THROW A BOMB AT IT!!
SHA

OOPS, WRONG ONE!!
PICKLED PLUMS
YOU'RE RIDICU-LOUS!!
SLURP

WRIGGLES
SOOOOUUUUR
THAT'S WORKING TOO?!!

IT LET GO OF ME!!
Was it really the pickled plum?!
CATCH!
TOSS
HA.

HOW'S ...
... THIS!!
SPLAT

YEEAAAH!!

URRGH
...
WE GOT ONE OF THE ZAPFISHES BACK!!

ZZZTZZZT
ZZT
DJ...?
AAAAAH!
SNEAK!
I HAVE TO REPORT THIS TO THE DJ!!
TCH
SHE ESCAPED.

SHWIP
OL' MAN, WE DID IT!!

HELP MEEEEE!
!
OH? HE'S NOT HERE.
?

U...
WOO
UFO ?!!
WOO
HE'S BEING CAP-TURED!!
I WANT TO RIDE THE UFO TOO!
So cool!
WHAT ?!
AGENT 3! AND AGENT 3.5!!
OL' MAN!!

GRRGH ...
SHUP
HAND OVER DA ZAPFISH, AND I'LL DROP THIS GUY LIKE A FRESH BEAT.

LET GO OF THE OL' MAN!!
OWWW!
DIDN'T YOU HEAR ME?!
LET GO!
YOU'LL PULL HIS LEG OFF!
ZWOO
AH... FORGET IT.
WHAT?
HUH?

SH
AAAAAAAH!!
ZWOOOO
!
DON'T YOU DARE LET GO!!
I'M GOING TO FALL!
UH, DID GRAMPS JUST GET KID-NAPPED?!
And, um...
WHO WAS THAT DANGLING FROM HIS FEET?

#8:HERO MODE
PART 2

GOGGLES AND RIDER HAVE TRAVELED BENEATH INKOPOLIS TO OCTO VALLEY...
...WHERE THEY MET CAP'N CUTTLEFISH.

IN ORDER TO GET THE GREAT ZAPFISH BACK...
...THE TWO OF THEM MUST NOW FIGHT THE OCTARIAN ARMY.
SOMEHOW, THEY MANAGED TO RETRIEVE ONE OF THE STOLEN ZAPFISH!
BUT THEN...
CAP'N CUTTLEFISH WAS ABDUCTED BY A MYSTERIOUS UFO...!
AND SO...

ZOOOM
WHAT NOW ?!
THE OCTOPUS WORLD IS FUN.
MUNCH MUNCH
HOW CAN YOU EAT RIGHT NOW?!
SHH

ZWOO
MUNCH MUNCH
I DIDN'T FINISH MY LUNCH EARLIER, SO...
THIS ISN'T AN OUTING, YOU KNOW!
OO
YAP YAP
Grrgh...
I CAN'T TAKE THESE GUYS...

ZIG
EAT THIS!
HAND OVER DA ZAPFISH!
NO!
AAAAAAH!!
ZIG

BUT YOU CAN HAVE MY OMELET!
It's the last one!
OMELET?! ARE YOU SCRAMBLED?

SPLO
SHW
I'MA DUB-STOMP YOU HARD!
AAAAH !!
OO
SH

WHOOAA!
SHWIIP
!

SHU
ZZT
GRRGH.
ZZT
!
THE GREAT ZAPFISH!!
ZZT ZZT
AND THAT'S THE LEADER OF THE OCTARIANS...

BAAAA
DJ OCTAVIO !!
MWA HA HA...
I'MA MAKE YOU *TREMOLO* IN FEAR...!!

BAAAM
WASABI?
...!
OONTZ
OONTZ
MUSIC ?!
HOW'S THAT SUPPOSED TO FILL US WITH FEAR?
OONTZ
OONTZ
OONTZ
NICE. NICE.
Aw, yeeaah.
STOP DANCING !!
OONTZ
COOOOL, A ROBOT!!
THIS ISN'T THE TIME FOR THAT!!
NICE...
KR CHK

BOO
NOT COOL!
OSH
OONTZ OONTZ
D-D-D-DJ OCTAVIO!
ZSH
ZSH
MWA HA HA.
DA POWER OF DA BEATS MAKES ME STRONGER.

BOO
KRCHK
IT'S SO POWER-FUL!!
SH
HERE COMES THE RIGHT ARM!!
BA
AAAAH!!
WOOM

SHUSHKT
OONTZ OONTZ
AND ...
WHAT?
SHWING
ATTACK!!
BWO
HE'S GOING ALL OUT!!
OSH

BR
AKA-WOO
OM
THIS IS UNBELIEV-ABLE!!
AAAAAH!!
WUMP
!
WHOA?!
BAP
WHERE'D THEY COME FROM?!
TCH!
SPLUB SPLUB SPLUB
OOMTZ
OOMTZ
CHAAARGE!!

THERE'RE TOO MANY OF THEM! I CAN'T GET TO OCTAVIO!
WE'RE DONE FOR!!
ALL RIGHT.
LEAVE IT TO ME!
GLOMP
?!
AGENT 3?!
I SEE!
HE'S GOING TO RIDE THE FIST BACK UP TO OCTAVIO!!
FWOOOOO
OH MY!
WHAAAAAAAT!!

...
KRCHK
BOOSH
WHAT?

I'M BACK.
OOO
ZWSH
BUT WHY?!

AAAARGH !!
BA-WHUM
WHAT WAS THE POINT OF THAT?!
HOW DARE HE FRIGHTEN ME...!
TIME TO SPEED UP THE BEAT!!

OONTZ OONTZ
ZSH ZSH
THE OCTARIANS ARE GETTING STRONGER?!
THEY'RE SPEEDING UP!!
WHOA!
OONTZ OONTZ
THE WILDER AND FASTER DA BEAT...
...DA STRONGER DA OCTARIANS GET!!
ZZ SSH HH
OONTZ
GP
P
KEEP UP THE BEAT!!
AW, MAN!!

HUH?
ZS
SH

A RADIIIIIIIISH ?!!
WHERE ARE MAH WASABI ?!!

I SWITCHED THEM WHILE I WAS UP THERE!
WHY ?!
I CAN'T KEEP THE BEAT WITH THIS WATERY VEGETABLE!!
ZSSH
ZSSH
IT'S WORKING ?!

SWOOO
I like grated radish more.
Why'd you even have them on you?!
THE OCTARIANS HAVE SLOWED DOWN!
Now's our chance.
THERE'S STILL TOO MANY FOR THE THREE OF US!
IT'S FIVE!

SPLASH
WHO'S THAT?!
OOH!
THOSE ARE...
?!
INKZOOKA !!
BLA
AGENT 1!
AND AGENT 2!
THE HEROES MAKE A GRAND ENTRANCE AT THE LAST MOMENT!
HEROINES, ACTUALLY.
DOW!

THEY'RE AGENTS 1 AND 2?!
Cool!
THAT'S RIGHT!
My grand-daughters.
HUMPH.
YOU SHOULDN'T PUSH YOURSELF LIKE THIS, GRAMPS.
YOU'RE NOT AS YOUNG AS YOU USED TO BE.
SO MANY OCTARIANS TAKEN DOWN BY A SINGLE INKZOOKA SHOT...
WHO ARE THEY?
Okay!
THE NEW SQUIDBEAK SPLATOON IS ASSEMBLED!
LET'S DO IT!
TIME FOR A COUNTER-ATTACK!!
SPLUB
SPLUB
SPLUB
YEEAAAH!!

SHO
EAT THIS!
!
OM
SPLUB SPLUB
YEE-HAH!!
SPLUB SPLUB
LOOK OUT BELOW!
SHA
YAAH!
KER-
SPL
AT!
WHAT ?!
HER MOVES ARE AMAZING ...!!
COOOL!!
SHA
AA

BLA
M
BLAM
BLAM
BLAM
!
WATCH YOUR BACKS, BOYS.
HER SHOTS SO FAST AND PRECISE!
AND THAT FACE...
WOOOOW!
Thanks.
MAR... I MEAN, AGENT 2, LET'S GO!
OKAY.

SPLUB
SPLUB
SPLUB
WOW!
THEY WORK TOGETHER PERFECTLY!
THEY MIGHT BE *BETTER* THAN THE S4.
GRRGH...
YOU'RE STILL A GREAT SHOT! Nice!
You're not so bad yourself.
I'LL PROTECT YOUR BACK.
WE SHOULD DO THAT TOO!
I'll protect your back!
WHAT IS THIS SUP-POSED TO BE?!
Get off me!
SPLUB
HEY, THIS WORKS BETTER THAN I THOUGHT!!
LET'S TRY THEIR MOVE!
ABSO-LUTELY NOT.
SPLUB

SPLUB
LET'S GO TEAM!!
SPLUB
SPLUB
MY OCTARIANS HAVE FALLEN...
BUT I STILL HAVE MY GRAND FINALE...!
FINALE?
KWEE
EEE
KRR
RRR

RALLY MISSILE!!
BWOOSH
WHAAAAAT?!
YOU'RE DONE FOR!!
OH NO!!
GLOMP
AGAIN?!
I'LL CRASH INTO THE GROUND IF WE DON'T DO SOME-THING!
WHAT A DUMMY!

ZIP
F
F
TCH.
I KNOW!
?!
HIT THE BOMB BACK AT HIM!
LET'S DO IT!
OKAY!
TCH!
KRRRR
THWACK
!

IT WORKED!!
GET HIM, AGENT 3!!
NOOOOOOO!!

YEEAAH!!

KA-BLAM!
WO
HURRAAAAY!!

THIS SHOULD DO THE TRICK.
HE'LL STAY TRAPPED IN THERE AS LONG AS I KEEP AN EYE ON HIM.
GRRGH.
WHY DID YOU STEAL THE GREAT ZAPFISH IN THE FIRST PLACE?
...

OCTO VALLEY DOESN'T HAVE ENOUGH ELECTRICITY.
WE HAD TO STEAL 'EM TO KEEP DA BEATS BUMPIN'...
I SEE...

LET'S GIVE THEM SOME!
WHAT ?!

SOME OF THE ZAPFISH ?!
INKOPOLIS HAS PLENTY OF ELECTRICITY, BUT...
IS THAT OKAY?
With you and your friends?

ALL RIGHT!
You can each take turns generating the electricity.
YOU...
NOD NOD
LOOKS LIKE EVERYTHING HAS BEEN SETTLED.
WE'LL BE OFF, THEN.
!
THUK
AAAH!
FWUMP
ARE YOU ALL RIGHT ?!
OOOPS.
BAAM
WE MESSED UP.
WHAT?
THE SQUID SIS...
...TERS ?!
SH
UP

SHHH.
DON'T TELL ANY-ONE!

SPLISH
OKAY, I WON'T!
Bye-bye.
I HAD A HUNCH BUT...
How strong are they?
YOU WANNA BUY THEIR NEW CD?
I'll give you an agent discount.
WHAT?! NO!!

BYE, OL' MAN AND DJ!!
I'll be back soon!
THANKS FOR EVERY-THING.
KLANK
OH!

IT'S THE GREAT ZAPFISH!!
It's come back!
GREAT JOB, TEAM!

#10:GLOVES

TURF WAR!!

SPECIAL WEAPON
INKZOOKA !!
AAAAAH!!

NICE!!
OKAY. HERE I GO AGAIN.
Zzz zzz...
GOG-GLES...
GOG-GLES!
THIS IS TEAM BLUE, THE PRIDE OF INKOPOLIS.
HEAD-PHONES
SPECS
BOBBLE HAT

WAKE UP!!
IT'S TIME FOR OUR TURF WAR!!
Stop dreaming!
He's sleeping standing up!
ZZZ...
THEY'RE ALSO FAMOUS FOR BEING RIDICULOUS.

WHAT?
BUT I'M IN A TURF WAR RIGHT NOW.
WE HAVEN'T EVEN STARTED YET!!
Put me down!
AH!!
HURRAY! I GET TO PLAY TURF WAR AGAIN!
Again?
WHAT'S WRONG WITH YOU?!

I FORGOT MY WEAPON...
YOU DOO-FUS!!
Oops.
TEAM BLUE, RIDICULOUS AS EVER.
Oh.
A TEXT MESSAGE FROM JUNGLE HAT.
HE GOT HIS FOOT STUCK IN HALF-DRIED CONCRETE, SO HE CAN'T COME.
WHAA-AAAT?!!
WAAAH!
HOW CAN I PLAY WITHOUT A WEAPON?!
Dummy!
THEY'RE BOTH HOPE-LESS.
WAAAH!
AAAAH!
I'LL LEND YOU MY SHOOTER.
!

SWIP
ZUFFF
THIS SWEET SHOOTER, RIGHT HERE.

WHO'S THAT?
WHAT'S WITH THAT HAIR-STYLE?!
I'VE NEVER SEEN HIS WEAPON OR GEAR BEFORE!
COOL!!

I'M GLOVES!
MY WEAPON AND GEAR ARE THE LATEST MODELS.
MY HAIRSTYLE IS THE LATEST TREND TOO.
LATEST TREND...? WELL, IT IS KINDA COOL...

I CAN GIVE YOU ONE!
VRRRRRN
DON'T EVEN THINK ABOUT IT!
Put that away!

HERE YOU GO.
THANKS!!
AND IF YOU NEED A PLAYER, I CAN JOIN.
REALLY?!
NOW WE CAN START THE TURF WAR!!
YOU'RE A NICE GUY!!
WELL...

I'LL DEFINITELY BE A PLUS TO TEAM GREEN.
CUZ I'VE GOT BOTH SKILL AND LOOKS.
AND IT LOOKS LIKE YOU GUYS ARE FRESH OUT OF BOTH.
THAT WEAPON.
I'VE NEVER SEEN IT BEFORE...
WE'RE GONNA WIN!!
That guy's annoying!
FOR ONCE, WE AGREE.
LET'S GO!

IN TURF WAR...
Okay, okay.
...THE TEAM THAT USES THEIR WEAPON TO PAINT THE MOST SURFACE AREA WILL WIN!
The play-by-play report will be brought to you by the Squid Sisters.
YOU'LL HAVE AN ADVANTAGE HERE IN BLACKBELLY SKATEPARK IF YOU CAN HOLD THE HIGH GROUND IN THE CENTER!
TEAM GREEN
TEAM BLUE
TEAM BLUE
TEAM GREEN
READY...

SPLUB SPLUB
GO!!
GO, GO!!
GET TO THE HIGH GROUND!
A FURIOUS BATTLE HAS ALREADY BROKEN OUT IN THE CENTER OF THE STAGE!!
SPLUB SPLUB SPLUB
I WON'T LOSE!!
I WON'T EITHER!

Have you put deter-gent in it?
NOT TO A WASHING MACHINE!!
IT'S A SLOSHING MACHINE!!
And no, of course not!
HUURGH!
TEAM BLUE HAS THE LEAD!!
SPLUB SPLUB
KEEP IT UP!
KCH
BUT YOU WON'T GET ME.
NOT BAD.
Hmm.
SPLUB
SPLUB
AW, MAN!
JUST KIDDING ...
SHOOT!
SH
F
AN ATTACK FROM BOTH SIDES!
OOOOH.
DON'T FORGET ABOUT US!

RATATATATA
AAAAAH!!
WHAT?
HIT!!
WHAAT?!
I SAID YOU WON'T GET ME, DIDN'T I?
?!
TWO WEAPONS ?!
TWO GUNS ?!

COOL, HUH?
INTRODUCING THE SPLAT DUALIES.
IT'S A NEW WEAPON TYPE.
WOW!
OKAY, BRING IT ON!!
SPLUB SPLUB SPLUB
GOGGLES SEEMS TO HAVE THE DROP ON HIS OPPONENT!!
HMM, NOT BAD.
NOW, LET ME SHOW YOU JUST HOW COOL MY DUALIES CAN BE.
BWOO
SH

SHWOOM
!
SPLATATA
AAAAAAH!!

GOGGLES!
FWOOSH
!
RATATAT
AAAAH!!
EVERY TEAM BLUE MEMBER HAS BEEN HIT!!
THE MOBILITY OF THE SPLAT DUALIES IS UNBELIEVABLE!!
AND HE WIELDS HIS WEAPON LIKE A MASTER!!
FWIP
WOW...
SPLUB SPLUB
URRGH, IT'S NOT OVER YET!!
OOPS.

WELL, I'VE GOT THIS COVERED TOO.
CHK
SPECIAL WEAPON

SHOOOM
KRRR
WH...
TENTA MISSILES!!
WHAT IS THAT ?!

AAAAAARGH!!
HIT!!
I'VE NEVER SEEN ANYTHING LIKE THAT BEFORE!
A NEW SPECIAL WEAPON?!
THE CROWD IS HEATING UP!
HMM...

I CAME TO INKOPOLIS TO SEE ITS FAMOUS BLUE TEAM IN ACTION.
BUT THERE'S *NOTHING FRESH* ABOUT YOU GUYS.
NEW GEAR.
NEW WEAPONS.
NEW SPECIALS.
YOU HAVE TO FOLLOW THE LATEST TRENDS...
...IF YOU WANNA BE THE COOLEST.

SLAP
AAAAAAH
BZZZZZZ

FWUMP

M...
MY FRESH NEW HAIR-STYLE?!

O-OH MY!
PART OF HIS HOT, TRENDY HAIRSTYLE HAS BEEN SHAVED RIGHT OFF!
Your head looks cool.
GLOVES SEEMS ABSOLUTELY SHOCKED!!
Aaaah!
SORRY!
MAYBE IT'LL STICK BACK ON?!
IT WON'T STICK BACK ON!
L...
L...

SPLUBSPLUBSPLUB
LET'S JUST STAY COOL!!!
Whooaa!
HE'S NOT STAYING COOL AT ALL!!
Every-body run!
TAKE THIS!!
SPLUB
FOR SOME REASON HE'S SHOOTING AT THE BALLOON!!
OH?
UM, I THINK HE'S LOST HIS MARBLES.
NOW'S OUR CHANCE!!

PAINT!
PAINT!
SPLUB
SPLUB
SPLUB
SPIN
HA HA HA
SPLUB SPLUB
SPIN
PAINT EVERY-THING!!
WHAAAAAT?!
AAAH!
WHAT A POWERFUL TEAM ATTACK!
HAHAHA
GET AWAY FROM THE HIGH GROUND!!
AAAH!
KWEEE

BLA
I'M OVER HERE TOO!
AIYEEE!!
NICE!!
YOU TOO!
ACK!
TEAM BLUE IS GOING WILD!!
SPLUB SPLUB
SHPING
WHAT? WE'RE LOSING?!
BUT THAT'S NOT COOL!
LOOK WHO'S TALKING!!

HERE IT GOES!
ACK!!
GOGGLES IS GOING TO USE INKZOO-KA!!
HIDE BEHIND THAT TOWER!!
NO!!
NOT INK-ZOOKA!
THE SPECIAL WEAPON OF THAT SPLATTER-SHOT IS...!!
WHAT?!

STING RAY!!

WHAT?! THE INK SHOT OUT LIKE A LASER BEAM...!!
IT WENT STRAIGHT THROUGH THE TOWER WALL?!
WOOOOW!!
THIS ISN'T...
...COOL!!
AAAAH!
BEEEEP
GAME SET!!

WA
AH
TEAM BLUE WINS!!
WE DID IT!!
Meow!!
We lost again!
THIS IS SOOOO FUN!!
AAAH, EEEK!
STOP IT!!
STOP PLAYING AROUND!
YEEAAAH!
GLOVES, THANKS A LOT FOR THE WEAPON!
Here.
HUMPH
Hey, your hair's back.
YEAH.
I used some bobby pins.
THIS NEW WEAPON IS REALLY IMPRES-SIVE!!
!
IT IS, ISN'T IT?

THIS IS THE LATEST MODEL OF SPLATTER-SHOT.
WEAPONS, GEAR, SPECIALS, EVEN STAGES...
THERE ARE LOTS OF NEW TRENDS HITTING THE SCENE.
REALLY ?!
MORE NEW STUFF MEANS...
...THE BATTLES WILL BE EVEN MORE FUN!
!

THEY DON'T EVEN CARE ABOUT NEW TRENDS AND FRESH STYLES. THEY JUST LOVE THE JOY OF BATTLES...
I can't wait!

NOW THAT'S COOL!

YOU SHOULD COME BY MY PART OF TOWN SOME TIME.
I'm cold?
He's saying you're impressive.

INKOPOLIS SQUARE!

INKOPOLIS SQUARE?
THAT'S NOT TOO FAR FROM HERE AT THE PLAZA.

YOU'LL MEET MORE COOL TREND FOLLOWERS LIKE ME...
...ENJOYING HOT NEW TURF WARS DOWN THERE.
SEE YOU AT INKOPOLIS SQUARE!
YOU BET! WE'LL DEFINITELY BE THERE!!

#11:SQUARE

WE'RE HERE!
INKOPOLIS SQUARE!!
WOW! IT'S FULL OF TRENDY STUFF!
I CAN'T WAIT FOR OUR FIRST PRACTICE AT INKOPOLIS SQUARE!
WE'VE ALREADY BOUGHT NEW GEAR AND WEAPONS TOO.
BUT GOGGLES ISN'T HERE YET!!
Now, now.
CALM DOWN YOU GUYS.
HERE, TRY ONE.
It's good.
YOU'RE SO KIND!
SORRY I'M LATE!
Oh.
HE'S HERE!

BAAAM
I WAS GETTING A GOOD LOOK AROUND TOWN.
WHAT ARE YOU DOING WAY UP THERE?!
He's on top of the building!
IT WAS THE BEST VIEW!
I'M SURE!
BAAM
I'LL USE SUPER JUMP TO GET TO YOU.
WHAT?
FROM UP THERE ?!
BWOOOSH

BWO
OSH
OWW, HOT!
HE'S FLYING SO FAST, HE'S BURNING!!
SHOOOM
HE'S FLYING TOO FAST!!
KR RCH
CRAASH
I CAN'T STOP !!
HE CRASHED !!

ARE...
ARE YOU ALL RIGHT?!

I'M FINE. EVERY-THING'S FINE!!
HNNGH
MY FOOD TRUCK!!
Dummy. He's a dummy.
I'm stuck!
PSSSH
IT'S NOT FINE AT ALL!!
AAAH!
I'M SO SORRY!!
I MIGHT FORGIVE YOU, BUT PUT SOME CLOTHES ON FIRST!!
FWEEE
SORRY. THIS IS TAKING A WHILE.

I GOT MYSELF A COOL NEW SET OF GEAR!!
OOH
NICE. IT LOOKS GOOD ON YOU!!
Nice.
SO...
...WHAT ARE YOU GOING TO DO ABOUT MY TRUCK?
STARE
Ehhh...
MONEY, MONEY!!
TUMP
HOW MANY OF THOSE DOES HE HAVE? NOT A LOT OF APLOMB WITH THIS KID...
TUMP
AH!
WILL THIS DO?!
PICKLED PLU
Pickled Plum
NOT EVEN CLOSE!
WHAT SHOULD I DO?!
AAAAAAH!
I HAVE AN IDEA FOR YOU.
OH!

IT'S GLOVES!
HEY.
WELCOME TO INKOPOLIS SQUARE.

I'M SURE IT WAS FILLED WITH NEW TRENDS AND ITEMS THAT YOU'VE NEVER EVEN SEEN DOWN AT THE PLAZA.
GRRR
DO YOU ALWAYS HAVE TO BE SO IRRITATING?

HE WAS GREAT IN THE MATCH THOUGH.
HE MADE PERFECT USE OF THE SPLAT DUALIES.
Your hair grew back! I'm so glad.
Y-Yeah.

MY FOOD TRUCK...
GLARE
AAAAAH!
I FORGOT! WE DON'T HAVE TIME FOR SMALL TALK!!
WHAT IS THIS IDEA OF YOURS?
UH-HUH.

BA
SQUARE KING CUP
PRELIMINARY ROUND
THIS!
A TURF WAR TOURNAMENT ?!
YEAH.
YOU SHOULD ENTER IT.
This is only the preliminary round, though.

IT'S A LARGE YEARLY TOURNAMENT.
THE WINNER IS CROWNED THE *BEST* TEAM IN INKOPOLIS SQUARE!

B-BEST?!
SOUNDS FUN!!
I'VE ALREADY QUALIFIED IN ANOTHER PRELIMINARY TOURNAMENT BLOCK.

AND AS AN ADDED PRIZE, YOU CAN OPEN YOUR OWN COOL NEW SHOP IN INKOPOLIS SQUARE!
WE'LL BE ABLE TO PAY BACK CRUSTY SEAN!!
THAT'S IT!!

THANKS, GLOVES!!
ST
RIP
THAT'S NO WAY TO SHOW YOUR GRATITUDE!!
THAT WASN'T COOL!!
YAP
I'LL GO SIGN US UP.
THE NEXT BATTLE WILL BE TEAM BLUE FROM INKOPOLIS PLAZA...
MRMR
MRMR
OH.
IT'S US!
...AGAINST...

BA
AM
...TEAM HOCKEY!!
...FROM INKOPOLIS SQUARE!!
A FRESH NEW TEAM THAT'S AT THE TOP OF EVERYONE'S PICK 'EM LIST.
HA HA.
THE LEADER OF THE TEAM IS HOCKEY!
THEY HAVEN'T LOST A SINGLE MATCH IN THE PRELIMINARY ROUNDS YET!!
What?!
THEY'RE A STRONG TEAM!!
AND WE JUST BOUGHT OUR NEW WEAPONS!
We haven't even practiced with them yet.
WE'RE IN TROUBLE!!

LUCKY US. THEY LOOK LIKE A WEAK TEAM.
THEY'RE NOT USED TO THEIR WEAPONS EITHER. THIS SHOULD BE EASY.
YEAH, A PIECE OF CAKE.
HUMPH.

DON'T WORRY. DON'T WORRY!
LET'S MAKE SURE WE HAVE FUN FIRST AND FOREMOST!

!
RIGHT!
I CAN'T WAIT!!
I WONDER WHAT THE STAGE WILL BE LIKE!
You can try out a bunch of new weapons too.
Yeah!
HUH?
THEY GOT THEIR SPIRIT BACK ALREADY.
NO PROBLEM.

AFTER ALL, WE'VE GOT OUR *INVINCIBLE FORMATION.*
GRIN

This is the play-by-play report seat.
IN A TURF WAR...
...THE TEAM THAT USES THEIR WEAPONS TO PAINT THE MOST SURFACE AREA WILL WIN!
PRELIMINARY ROUND
TEAM BLUE (INK COLOR: BLUE)
TEAM HOCKEY (INK COLOR: ORANGE)
THE REEF IS A STAGE WITH ATTACK LANES IN EVERY DIRECTION!
READY...
THIS IS OUR...
...FIRST BATTLE IN INKOPOLIS SQUARE!!
B-BMP
B-BMP

SPLUB SPLUB SPLUB
GO!!
SPLUB SPLUB
LET'S HAVE FUN!
EH!
IT'S OUR FIRST TIME HERE. I DON'T KNOW WHICH ROUTE TO TAKE!!
AAAAH!
SPLUB SPLUB
Trouble!
WE HAVEN'T TALKED OUT A PLAN EITHER!
C-C-C-CALM DOWN!
UHHHH
TAKE YOUR OWN ADVICE!
LET'S SPLIT UP AND PAINT THE STAGE FIRST!

SPLUB SPLUB SPLUB
YEEAAH!!
TEAM BLUE HAS SPLIT UP TO PAINT THE STAGE WITH INK!!
GRIN
SPLUB SPLU
SHA
A
NOW YOU'RE ALL ALONE!
!
I'VE BEEN SURROUND...
SPLUB
...ED!!
SPECS!
SPLUB
NEXT!
AIYEEE!
SHF
HIT!!
SP LUB

TEAM BLUE MEMBERS ARE FALLING ONE BY ONE!!
EVERY-ONE!
THEY'RE ALREADY IN TROUBLE!!
THIS BATTLE MIGHT BE DIFFICULT FOR THEM.
SPLUB
TEAM HOCKEY TAKES THE LEAD WITH EASE!
SPLUB
Ha ha!
WHAT DO YOU THINK OF THIS PERFECT FORMA-TION?
UH-OH!
IT'S CALLED...
4DS!!
4DS ?!

BAAM
IT'S THE 4 OF US ARE DEAD SHOTS!!
Shots...
Shots...
Shots...
THAT'S SO HOKEY!!
HUUH ?!
COOOOOL !!
AT LEAST ONE OF YOU'S A NICE GUY!
BUT...

...THIS IS THE END OF THE LINE FOR YOU!!
SPLUB SPLUB
TAKE THIS! 4DS!!
SPLUB SPLUB
!
SPLUB
4DS!
4DS!
GOGGLES IS TRAPPED! HE'S IN BIG TROUBLE!!
SPLUB
SPLUB
WHOOAA!
GOGGLES!
USE SUPER JUMP TO ESCAPE!!
OKAY!
SWSH
YOU'RE STAYING RIGHT HERE!!
VWSH
!

OOPS.

FWUMP
HOCK-EEEEY!!
OOOOOOH
THAT HAS GOT TO BE PAINFUL.
I'd imagine.
AAAAH!
ARE YOU ALL RIGHT?!
Sorry! Accident!
POOR GUY...
That had to hurt...
HOW DARE YOU...
STAGGER
ARE YOU OKAY?!
YEAH, LET'S GO!
SHFF
4DS OF ANGER!!
THEY'RE SO FAST!!
VSH
OKAY!
WE'LL USE OUR FORMATION TOO!!
What?
WE HAVE A FORMATION?

BAAAAM
BLUE SQUID ACROBAT TEAM!!
HUUURGH
WHAT IS THAT ?!
KRRRASH
WAAAH!
OH, NO! WE'RE FALLING!!
THAT'S WHAT I THOUGHT !!
HUMPH.

BLAA
I'LL JUST FIGHT AWESOME, LIKE ALWAYS!
?!
WE LOST ONE!
SHE'S A GOOD SHOT !!
SWEE

SLISH
NICE!
YOU CAN'T LET YOUR GUARD DOWN.
SPLOSH
SHFF
DID SHE SWIM OVER HERE ON THE CHARGER'S INK STREAM?!
NICE!
I'LL ATTACK TOO!!
SPLUUB
WHEN DID HE GET BEHIND ME?!
YAAAH!
NO ONE WAS WATCHING ME!!
Isn't someone going to say "nice"?!
WHAT IS THIS?!
THEY'RE RIDICU-LOUS BUT THEY'RE GOOD?!
I'VE NEVER HEARD OF TEAM BLUE IN INKOPOLIS!
THE ONLY INKLINGS I'VE HEARD OF ARE THE S4...!
APPARENTLY, THEY DEFEATED THE S4.
WHAAAAAT?!

I WASN'T TOLD THEY WERE...
...THAT STRONG !!
SPLUB
OKAY.

SPLUB
KEEP ATTACKING!!
THEY REALLY ARE AN ABSURD TEAM.
GAME SET!!
AND THE RESULT IS...?!

SHA
TEAM BLUE WINS!!
WAAH!
AW, MAN!!
TURF WAR BATTLES ARE SO FUN!
RIGHT ON!
UH-HUH!
All right.
LET'S KEEP ROLLING RIGHT THROUGH THESE PRELIMS!
SECOND MATCH
TEAM BLUE WINS!!
THIRD MATCH
TEAM BLUE WINS!!

TEAM BLUE HAS WON THEIR PRELIMINARY ROUND...
...AND MADE IT INTO THE MAIN ROUND!!
WAAH
HURRAY!!
CON-GRATS.
AND THERE'S SOMEONE ELSE I WANT TO FIGHT TOO.
WHAT?
WE MAY END UP AGAINST EACH OTHER IN THE MAIN ROUND.
But I won't lose again.
UH...

99.9%
0.1%
THE EMPEROR.
BBLLL

FOUR-TIME WINNER AND ABSOLUTE CHAMPION.

DON'T FEEL BAD ABOUT LOSING.
THE EMPEROR *ALWAYS* PREVAILS.
NINETY-NINE-POINT-NINE PERCENT COVERAGE?!!
NI...
YOU'LL HAVE TO BEAT HIM TO GET THE SQUARE KING CUP.
...

SOUNDS LIKE FUN!!
W-WE WON'T LOSE!!
AWESOME!
HOPE TO SEE YOU GUYS IN THE NEXT ROUND THEN!
YOU CAN COUNT ON IT!
LET'S WIN THAT CUP!!
GOOD LUCK!

THE BONUS MANGA
WILL START ON
THE NEXT PAGE!

INKOPOLIS PLAZA
I CALL THIS BATTLE TEAM MEETING TO ORDER!
BONUS: TEAM MEETING
OOOOH
LOOK AT ALL THESE FANCY DRINKS.
WAAH WAAH
Yeah.
TALK ABOUT CHOICES!!
WHAT SHOULD I GET...
I'LL ORDER FIRST!

CARAME ...
CARAMEL FRAPPERI ...
...FRAP-PUCCI...
KRNCH
HE BIT HIS TONGUE!!
Or maybe he just can't pronounce it
BAM
ROASTED GREEN TEA!!
NO WAY THEY HAVE THAT!!
What an old fashioned choice.
ssss
HERE YOU ARE.
HURRAY!
THEY ACTUALLY HAVE IT?!
HEY, KEEP IT DOWN.
Of course it's them.
RIDER!!
WELL, WELL.

BAAM
IF IT AIN'T TEAM BLUE!!
EWW
THE S4 ARE HERE TOO ?!
WHY ARE YOU GUYS ALL HERE TOGETHER?!
TCH!
PURE COINCI- DENCE.
OH, WE'RE...
HEY...!
WE JUST HAPPENED TO BE HERE. NOTHING PLANNED.
YOU'RE ALL SUCH GOOD FRIENDS.
GLARE
NO WAY.
SCARY !!
Eeek.

I'm outta here.
Wait! Let's have tea together!
AAAAAH!
SH
UP
That goof!
WHA?!

...
WHAT'S WRONG, HEAD-PHONES?
I'VE ALWAYS WONDERED, DO SPECS' SPECS EVEN HAVE LENSES?
His eyes are always popping through them.
THUNGKT
Aaah!
NOW THAT YOU MENTION IT...
SHF

LET'S SEE!
KRASH

THEY SURE DO!
I wonder how it works then.
HOW WHAT WORKS?!
AAAAARGH!!
Oooh.
SPECS !!
Geez,
down.

Let's pull ourselves together...
TIME FOR THE MEETING!
LET US GIVE YOU SOME ADVICE.
THE S4?!
THE BLEND OF THE SPICES IS IMPORTANT, BUT DON'T FORGET ABOUT THE STEW.
CURRY MANUAL
WE'RE NOT TALKING ABOUT CURRY!
EVERYONE LIKES TO HEAR A COMPLIMENT ABOUT THEIR FINER QUALITIES. EVERYONE. ♪
WE'RE NOT TALKING ABOUT HOW TO HIT ON GIRLS EITHER!!
We're talking about Turf Wars!
HYUK HYUK
DID YOU SERIOUSLY THINK I'D GIVE ADVICE TO AN ENEMY?
NO, I DIDN'T!
BAAM
LEAVE ME ALONE.
THAT'S HUGE!!
I guess he has a sweet tooth, huh?
SHUP
AH!
WILL WE GET TO SEE HIS FACE?!

SHOOM
EMPTY
THAT WAS FAST!!

WOOOOW!!
HOW DO YOU DO THAT?!
FIRST, YOU MAINTAIN STEADY BREATHING AND...
YOU'RE ACTUALLY GOING TO TEACH HIM?!

SHOOOM
I CAN DO IT TOO.
NOW YOU'RE
?!
Wow, Rider!
GWOOO
YEAH, LET'S HAVE A COMPETITION!!
WHAAT?!

THREE HOURS LATER
I'M SO FULL...
This was not a good idea!
Tch.
WE'VE ALL EATEN WAY TOO MUCH!!
AH!
AND WE HAVEN'T EVEN TALKED ABOUT OUR STRATEGIES YET!!
BURP
OOPS!!
BONUS: TEAM MEETING / END

INKLING ALMANAC

MODE ARC

Weapon: Hero Shot
Headgear: Pilot Goggles + Hero Headset
Clothing: Hero Jacket
Shoes: Hero Runner

GOGGLES

HERO

Weapon:	Hero Roller
Headgear:	Hero Headset
Clothing:	Hero Jacket + Black Inky Rider
Shoes:	Hero Runner

RIDER

MODE ARC

AGENT 1

Weapon: Hero Roller

AGENT 2

Weapon: Hero Charger

The Squid Research Lab created special research material for me to use in the manga!

GLOVES

Weapon: Splat Dualies
Headgear: Squidfin Hook Cans
Clothing: Black V-Neck Tee
Shoes: Yellow-Mesh Sneakers

INFO

• He spends an hour doing his hair each day.
• Every morning, he practices his cool poses in the mirror.

HOCKEY

Weapon:	Splattershot
Headgear:	Hockey Helmet
Clothing:	Dark Urban Vest
Shoes:	Black Trainers

INFO

• He came up with 4DS in the shower and was so excited he couldn't sleep that night.

STRIPED BEANIE

Weapon:	N-ZAP '89
Headgear:	Striped Beanie
Clothing:	Zekko Hoodie
Shoes:	Blue Slip-Ons

VADER CAP

Weapon:	Splattershot
Headgear:	Squidvader Cap
Clothing:	Red Tentatek Tee
Shoes:	Gray Sea-Slug Hi-Tops

HEADBAND

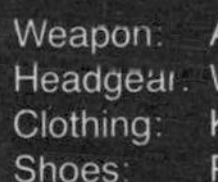

Weapon:	Aerospray MG
Headgear:	White Headband
Clothing:	King Jersey
Shoes:	Purple Hi-Horses

INFO

• Hockey is the one who came up with the name for the 4DS, but all his teammates like it.

TEAM HOCKEY

NEW TEAM BLUE

Weapon: Splattershot
Headgear: Pilot Goggles
Clothing: Eggplant Mountain Coat
Shoes: Hero Runner Replica

GOGGLES

BOBBLE HAT

Weapon: Slosher
Headgear: Bobble Hat
Clothing: Gray Hoodie
Shoes: Purple Sea Slugs

HEADPHONES

Weapon: Splat Charger
Headgear: Studio Headphones
Clothing: Slash King Tank
Shoes: Red Hi-Horses

SPECS

Weapon: Octobrush
Headgear: Retro Specs
Clothing: Baby-Jelly Shirt & Tie
Shoes: Smoky Wingtips

This is Team Blue created with the CG from the game. This is rare!

ANNOUNCEMENT MANGA THAT RAN IN JAPAN TO PROMOTE WHEN THE SERIES STARTED SERIALIZATION IN MONTHLY COROCORO MAGAZINE!

EMERGENCY ANNOUNCEMENT!!

FOR MORE BATTLES !!
PAINT AWAY!!
SPLUBSPLU

Splatoon
STORY & ART BY
SANKICHI HINODEYA
ARE YOU STUPID ?!
MY CLOTHES FELL OFF AGAIN!!
SERIES STARTS IN THE JUNE ISSUE OF MONTHLY COROCORO MAGAZINE.
Please read it!

Splatoon 3
THANK YOU!

The story enters a new arc!
Sankichi Hinodeya

Volume 3
VIZ Media Edition

Story and Art by
Sankichi Hinodeya

Translation **Tetsuichiro Miyaki**
English Adaptation **Jeremy Haun & Jason A. Hurley**
Lettering **John Hunt**
Design **Shawn Carrico**
Editor **Joel Enos**

Original Design **100percent**

Printed in Canada

Published by VIZ Media, LLC
P.O. Box 77010
San Francisco, CA 94107

10 9 8 7 6 5 4 3
First printing, June 2018
Third printing, October 2020

PARENTAL ADVISORY
SPLATOON is rated A and is
suitable for readers of all ages.

Splatoon reads from right to left!
This is the end of this graphic novel.